But I Just Can't Sleep!

Edith Faye Chester

Illustrated by: Bonnie Lemaire

Tellwell Talent
www.tellwell.ca

ISBN
978-0-2288-0495-6 (Paperback)

Note to Parents

The goal of this book is to enhance the bedtime experience for parents and children alike. It is based on a simple bedtime routine that I created for my own four lively children when all else failed in getting them to settle at night. Bedtime is one aspect of parenthood where children know exactly which buttons to push to cause tired parents to lose patience. Being put to bed with loving words and an "all is well" feeling versus harsh, angry words is critical for building self-esteem and security in a child.

The routine described in this book is based on stretching and relaxing muscles. Sleep experts tell us that doing this can relieve tension and promote relaxation for sleep. My own children and any child who stayed in our home loved this routine. However, it was really put to the test and shown to have great success when our teenaged daughter used it as a camp counsellor. Other counsellors would ask her how she settled her cabin so quickly at night.

The routine is a fun way to bring closure to a day and to help a child settle down for sleep. It can also help diffuse a potential conflict area (bedtime) between parent and child. I wish you well as you flop, wiggle, wave and stretch your way into an easier bedtime experience with your child.

Acknowledgments

This book would not have come about without the support of my loving family. My husband, Mark, and my mother, Marion Hunking, helped make this book a reality.

My children, Daniel, Timothy, Evangeline and Zachariah were the source of this bedtime routine. They have always pulled out the best in me. Their spouses, Jessica, Sarah and Tim are wonderful additions to the fabric of our family.

My grandchildren: Benjamin, Isabella, Elenora, Theodore, Elijah, Titus, Adelaide and Olivia continue to add to the "parade" of animals.

Dedication

It was my daughter, Evangeline Watson who picked up this project when I had given up. Vanje, your confidence in this idea and your search for the right publisher made this book happen. I have watched you encourage and champion so many people in your life and now, to my amazement, you have turned it on me, your mother! You were also the main reason floppsies was created. I dedicate this book to you.

But
I Just Can't
Sleep!

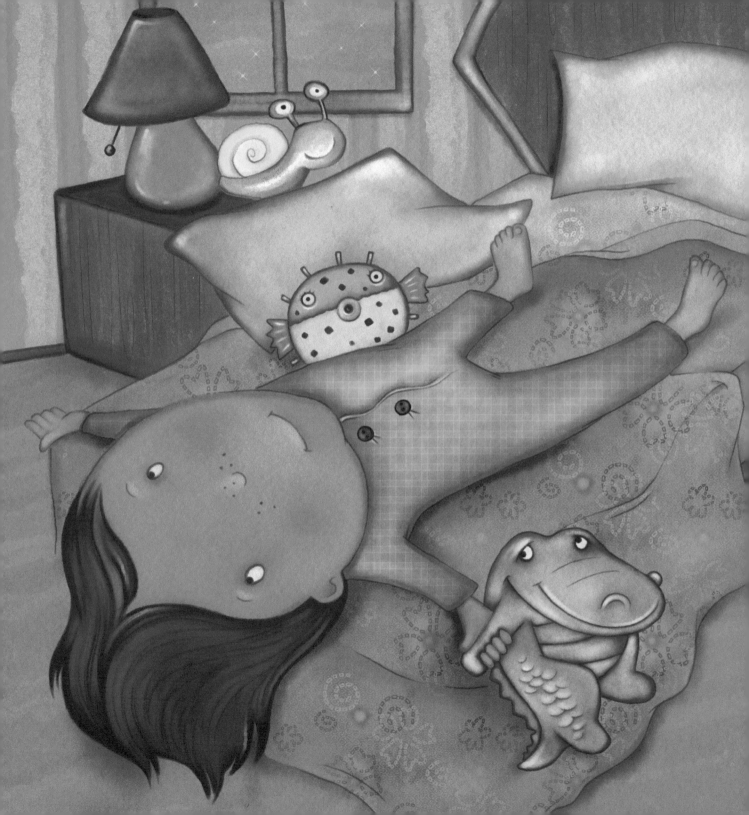

Sometimes it's hard
to go to bed.

Sometimes it's hard
to stay in bed.

Sometimes I just can't sleep.

Daddy tells me a story.

Mommy rubs my back and
sings. She says a prayer.

But I just can't sleep.

I go to the bathroom and sneak down the hall to see what everyone is doing.

Daddy says, "It's adult time now. YOU MUST GO TO SLEEP!"

"I can see you are not sleepy" says Mommy. "You may play quietly in your room."

I organize all my toys. I line up all my stuffies, like a parade on my bed. But I just can't sleep.

In a tired voice, Mommy says, "I have an idea. Let's do floppsies."

"Yes, yes!" I say, "Let's do floppsies!"

Mommy leans against the wall in the hall so my brothers can hear too. With a little smile on her face, she says, "O.K. Into bed you go. Lay on your back. The deal is no getting out of bed after floppsies. Agreed? Here we go..."

"First you flop one leg. Now flop your other leg."

Stomp your feet like an elephant.

Flop one arm. Flop
your other arm.

Snap your arms like a crocodile.

Now wave your arms
like a butterfly.

Flop your head. Flop your bum.

Now wiggle your
body like a worm.

Flop your knees from side to
side like a fish out of water.

Wave your arms and legs in the air like a monkey.

Now stretch...stretch...stretch...your arms and tippy toes as tall as a giraffe.

Curl up your legs and hug them in tight like a snail.

Breathe three deep breaths and puff out your chest like a puffer fish. One... two.... three...

Yawn like a lion.
Purr like a kitty cat.

Be quiet as a mouse
(squeak, squeak).

Close your eyes.
Smile a big smile.

Dream your favorite dreams.

Now go to sleep..."

"The animals are tired from doing all their stretches, Mommy. They are going to sleep, and I can too."

"Good night, my dear. I love you."

Mommy kisses me one last time. I close my eyes and...

...go to sleep.

CPSIA information can be obtained
at www.ICGtesting.com
Printed in the USA
LVHW070231120319
610315LV00002B/9/P

9 780228 804956